DOLPHMAN v.2

GREAT DAY FOR SAILING

CREATED AND WRITTEN BY

CURT THOMAS

ILLUSTRATED BY ZACHERY WIDEMAN

DOLPHMAN
WWW.DOLPHMAN.US

A SPECIAL THANK YOU
TO ALL HEALTHCARE PROFESSIONALS,
FIRST RESPONDERS AND ESSENTIAL WORKERS
FOR THEIR TIRELESS WORK AND SACRIFICE
DURING THE COVID-19 GLOBAL PANDEMIC.

DAVE WAS FEELING RESTLESS BEING IN NEW YORK CITY BECAUSE OF THE COLDER THAN NORMAL WINTER.

HE DECIDED THAT A TRIP TO THE CARIBBEAN MAY BE A GOOD WAY TO ESCAPE THE COLD AND GET A BIT OF SIGHTSEEING.

DAVE CHOSE THE ISLAND OF **TOBAGO** (TUH-BAY-GO).

ATLANTIC
E
W
S
DOMINICAN REP.
HAITI
PUERTO RICO
TOBAGO
CARIBBEAN
VENEZUELA

TRAVELING THROUGH THE CARIBBEAN,
DAVE STOPPED FOR
AN EXPLORATORY DIVE.

HIS OLD PAL, PHILLIP, CAUGHT UP
WITH HIM AS HE DROPPED
THE BOAT'S ANCHOR.

DAVE PULLED ON HiS BACKPACK
AND DOVE iNTO THE WATER.
AS HE HiT THE WATER,
HiS TRANSFORMATION WAS iNSTANT.

HE WAS **DOLPHMAN!**

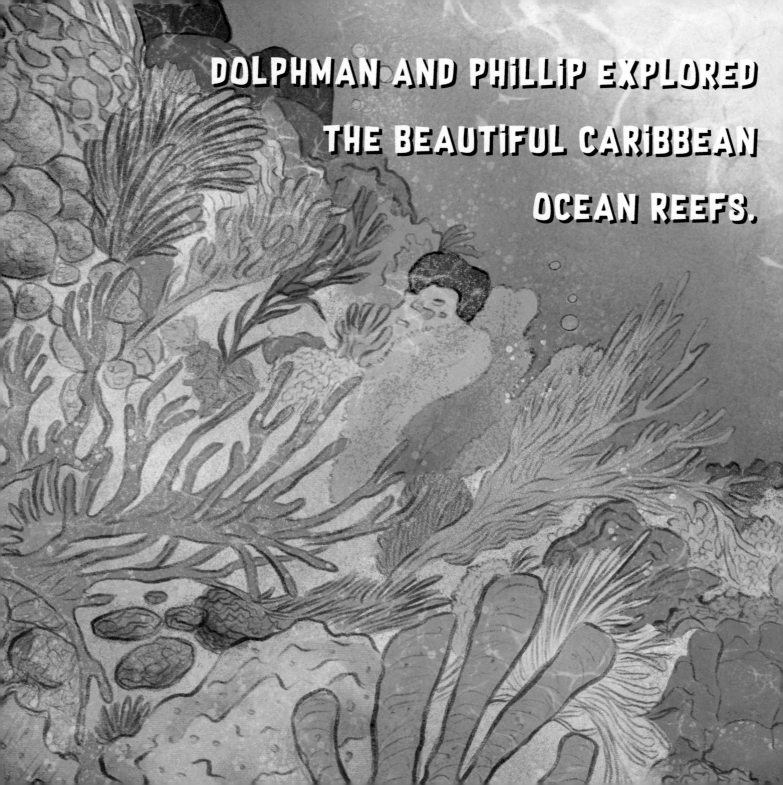

DOLPHMAN AND PHILLIP EXPLORED THE BEAUTIFUL CARIBBEAN OCEAN REEFS.

WHILE ON THEIR DIVE,

THEY CAME UPON A HUGE FIELD OF TIRES
THAT WERE INTENTIONALLY DISCARDED
IN THE OCEAN.

WHILE INVESTIGATING THE AREA, DOLPHMAN AND PHILLIP HEARD A CRY FOR HELP!

THEY FOUND A TURTLE ENTANGLED IN FISHING LINE, STUCK WITHIN THE MOUNTAIN OF TIRES.

DOLPHMAN GRABBED A TOOL FROM HIS BACKPACK, AND PROCEEDED TO UNTANGLE THE TURTLE.

"THANK YOU!" EXCLAIMED THE TURTLE IN RELIEF.

"MY NAME IS SEBASTIAN".

DOLPHMAN MADE A NOTE OF THE
LOCATION OF THE TIRES.

HE PLANNED TO NOTIFY THE AUTHORITIES
OF THE HARM BEING DONE TO THE OCEAN.
TOGETHER, THEY WOULD ORGANIZE
A CLEAN UP!

DOLPHMAN AND PHILLIP SAID
GOODBYE TO SEBASTIAN
AND CONTINUED ON THEIR TRIP.

ONCE OUT OF THE WATER AND BACK ON HIS BOAT, DOLPHMAN TRANSFORMED BACK TO DAVE.

AFTER A LONG TRIP ACROSS THE OCEAN, THEY FINALLY ARRIVED ON THE SHORES OF TOBAGO.

DAVE DOCKED HIS HOUSEBOAT AT A JETTY,
OFF THE BEACH OF PIGEON POINT.

AFTER A SHORT REST, DOLPHMAN AND PHILLIP
TOOK A DIVE AROUND THE REEF.
AMONG THE CORAL AND COLORFUL FISH,
THEY TOOK A SWIM TO THE NYLON POOL.

THEY ALSO EXPLORED A FEW WRECKS WITH ANCIENT ARTIFACTS.

IT WAS SUCH A BEAUTIFUL DAY, THE CHARLES FAMILY OF FOUR DECIDED TO TAKE THEIR BOAT FOR A SAIL.

THE FAMILY WAS A FEW MILES OFFSHORE, WHEN SUDDENLY THE WEATHER BEGAN TO CHANGE. FROM SUNNY TO RAINY, WITH STRONG WINDS AND LARGE WAVES.

MR. CHARLES SENT HIS FAMILY BELOW DECK. HIS SON CORI WAS FOLLOWING MRS. CHARLES, WHEN SUDDENLY THE MAST OF THE BOAT SWUNG AROUND, KNOCKING HIM OVERBOARD.

LUCKILY, CORi HAD ON HiS LiFEJACKET.

HE CRiED OUT FOR HELP,

BUT NO ONE HEARD HiM.

NO ONE EXCEPT FOR

DOLPHMAN!

AS HE EXPLORED THE REEFS WITH PHILLIP,
DOLPHMAN HEARD A CRY.
HE SUDDENLY STOPPED SWIMMING
AND TURNED AROUND.

HE MOTIONED TO PHILLIP AND THEY BOTH SWAM OFF AS FAST AS THEY COULD IN THE DIRECTION OF THE CRY FOR HELP!

DOLPHMAN AND PHiLLiP ARRiVED
AT THE BOY'S LOCATiON.
CORi WAS HAPPY TO SEE HiS RESCUERS.

DOLPHMAN STRAPPED CORi TO HiM
AND THEY FOLLOWED HiS FAMiLY'S BOAT
UNTiL iT CAME iNTO CALM WATERS.

CORI'S PARENTS WERE VERY THANKFUL.

FOR THEIR SON'S RETURN.

THE CHARLES FAMILY CONTINUED TOWARDS LAND.

THEY HAD ENOUGH ADVENTURE FOR ONE DAY.

DOLPHMAN GOT BACK TO HiS BOAT
AND AS HE CLiMBED ABOARD,
HE TRANSFORMED iNTO DAVE.

AFTER A LONG DAY, DAVE DECIDED TO GO ON LAND AND VISIT A LOCAL RESTAURANT.

THERE HE ENJOYED A RELAXED EVENING EATING ISLAND CUISINE AND LISTENING TO SWEET CALYPSO MUSIC WITH THE WARM, INVITING PEOPLE OF TOBAGO.

꧁ ~ **UNTIL NEXT TIME...** ~ ꧂

REVISIT PAST ADVENTURES FROM VOLUME 1

AND COMING SOON...

v.3

DOLPHMAN

THE BEGINNING

FOLLOW ON INSTAGRAM @DOLPHMANHERO
FOR UPDATES

THIS BOOK IS DEDICATED TO MY FIVE CHILDREN
WHO ENJOY VISITING THE ISLAND OF TOBAGO.
- CURT THOMAS, AUTHOR

Made in the USA
Middletown, DE
28 September 2023

39200580R00031